AR Quiz# 43684
BL: 4.2
AR Pts: 1.0

Sheltie™
Finds a Friend

Written and illustrated by **Peter Clover**

ALADDIN PAPERBACKS

New York   London   Toronto   Sydney   Singapore

First Aladdin Paperbacks edition September 2000

Copyright © 1996 by Working Partners Limited
First published 1996 by Penguin Books Limited
Created by Working Partners Limited

ALADDIN PAPERBACKS
An imprint of Simon & Schuster Children's Publishing Division
1230 Avenue of the Americas
New York, NY 10020

SHELTIE is a trademark owned
by Working Partners Limited.
All rights reserved, including the right of
reproduction in whole or in part in any form.
The text for this book was set in Sabon.
Printed and bound in the United States of America
2 4 6 8 10 9 7 5 3 1

Library of Congress Catalog Card Number 00-106715
ISBN 0-689-83975-8

*For Dorothy, Tony,
Sarah, and Miles*

Chapter One

It was a beautiful spring day in Little Applewood. Emma was in the paddock with Sheltie. They were playing Frisbee. Emma was trying to teach the little Shetland pony how to catch.

Sheltie was a clever pony and enjoyed

every minute of this new game. He wasn't very good at it, though. He couldn't catch for all the tea in China.

Emma threw the Frisbee and watched it sail through the air. The disc landed at Sheltie's feet, and the little pony gave a loud snort. He shook his long, shaggy mane.

Sheltie bent his head and picked up the Frisbee between his teeth. Then with a sudden flick, he tossed the plastic saucer up into the air.

Little Joshua was sitting on the paddock fence with Mom, watching the game. He clapped his hands together as Sheltie sent the Frisbee spinning over his head.

"Sheltie must be the only pony in the world who can do that," said Mom.

Emma took a roll of peppermints from

her jacket pocket and gave Sheltie one of his favorite treats.

"He's not very good at catching, though," said Emma. But it didn't matter. Sheltie was a pony, not a person. And Emma laughed each time he picked up the Frisbee and tossed it backward over his head.

★ ★ ★ ★ ★ ★ ★ ★

The very next morning, there was a surprise waiting for Emma down in the paddock.

Every day, the first thing Emma did when she woke up was to look at Sheltie out of her bedroom window. This morning when Emma looked, she could hardly believe her eyes.

As usual, Sheltie was standing by the paddock gate with his fuzzy chin resting on the top bar of the wooden fence. But standing there right next to him was a little black donkey.

Emma rubbed her eyes and looked again.

"Where did *he* come from?" Emma wondered. She pulled on her school uniform and hurried downstairs.

Mom and Dad were already sitting at the breakfast table. They were both wearing huge grins.

"Have you seen the donkey, Emma?" said Dad. "His name is Mudlark."

"Who does he belong to?" asked Emma. She couldn't wait to rush out to the paddock for a closer look.

Chapter Two

The little black donkey was almost the same size as Sheltie, but not quite as fat.

They stood side by side in the paddock, looking over the fence and up into the garden. When the donkey saw Emma, he threw back his head and brayed with a loud hee-haw.

Emma laughed and reached over to stroke Mudlark's furry head. His mane felt very bristly.

Sheltie gave a snort and nudged the donkey with his soft muzzle. Mudlark gave another bray, and his long ears waggled like a big rabbit's.

"Isn't he funny?" said Mom. She picked up Joshua so he could see better.

"Do you remember us telling you about Marjorie Wallace, Emma?" said Dad. "She's the lady who lives in the cottage at the foot of Beacon Hill."

Emma remembered. Marjorie Wallace had nine cats. She took in strays and found homes for unwanted kittens.

"Well, Mudlark belongs to Marjorie," said Mom. "The poor old lady hasn't had a vacation for ages. She doesn't like to leave her cats, so she never goes out of town."

"Marjorie has a sister," said Dad.

"And a brother somewhere," said Mom.

"Yes, but nobody knows much about him," said Dad. "Anyway, Marjorie hasn't seen her sister for six years. So all her friends in Little Applewood thought it would be a good idea if Marjorie went for a visit. And we're helping out by looking after Mudlark while she's away."

Emma thought this was a wonderful idea. And Sheltie thought it was fun, too. He snorted and gave Mudlark a gentle push. The little donkey brayed, then galloped around the paddock. Sheltie was close at his heels, playing chase.

"Who will take care of Marjorie's cats?" asked Emma.

"Mrs. Marsh is staying at the cottage while Marjorie's away. And the gardener said he would pop in from time to time to make sure everything is all right."

"One of Marjorie's cats has kittens, Emma. We thought you and Sheltie might like to ride over there after school to see them."

"Oh, yes, please," said Emma.

Joshua started to wriggle in Mom's arms. He wanted to go and see the kittens, too.

Emma unlocked the paddock gate and gave Sheltie and Mudlark their breakfast. Dad had put a bucket in Sheltie's field

shelter for Mudlark. The bucket was pushed tightly into an old car tire so it wouldn't get kicked over.

Emma stood back and watched Sheltie and Mudlark eat. They both gobbled down their breakfast in seconds.

Next, Emma filled the water trough with the hose. Mudlark blew bubbles in the water. Emma gave him a squirt and Mudlark threw back his head with a loud hee-haw. Sheltie answered with a loud snort and chased him across the paddock.

"I don't know which one is worse," laughed Mom. "Sheltie or Mudlark. I can see you're going to have your hands full this week, Emma!"

Chapter Three

After school, Emma rode Sheltie over to Marjorie Wallace's cottage at Beacon Hill. Emma was looking forward to seeing the kittens.

The cottage nestled at the foot of the hill, which was on the outskirts of town.

As Sheltie trotted along towards the cottage, Emma saw someone hop over Marjorie's low fence.

She had never seen this man before. He was quite old, dressed in rough-looking clothes, and he was carrying a sack. Emma was too far away to see him properly, but she watched as he disappeared into the woods behind the cottage. Maybe it was the gardener, she thought.

Emma dismounted and led Sheltie through the gate and up the path to the front door.

There was a big metal ring in the cottage wall. Emma tied Sheltie's rein to the ring and knocked on the red painted door.

Emma waited, but nobody came. She knocked again, louder this time, and heard footsteps inside. The cottage door swung open, and Mrs. Marsh stood on the front step.

"Hello," said Emma. "I've come to see the kittens." She gave Mrs. March her biggest smile.

"Oh dear," said Mrs. Marsh. "You'd better come in, Emma. You see, one of the kittens is missing. I can't find it anywhere. Perhaps you can help me find it."

Emma hunted high and low, all over the cottage. She looked in all the places she could think of where a kitten might hide.

She even looked outside, but there was no sign of the kitten anywhere.

"Perhaps it wandered off to explore," she said. "It'll come back when it's hungry. Cats always do."

"But it's so tiny," said Mrs. Marsh. "I don't know where it could have gone."

Emma stayed for half an hour and played with the other kittens. But when it was time to leave there was still no sign of the missing one.

As Emma and Sheltie rode away, Emma suddenly remembered the old man with the sack—the man she had seen hop over the fence and disappear into the woods.

I wonder what he had in that sack, thought Emma. Maybe it was the kitten!

* * * * * * * *

Back in the paddock, Dad was busy fitting Mudlark with a special harness. Emma's eyes grew wide as she watched Dad wheel a funny little cart out from behind Sheltie's field shelter.

Sheltie gave a loud snort and Mudlark answered with an even louder hee-haw.

"What's that for?" asked Emma. She jumped out of the saddle to take a better look.

The little cart was painted in bright colors, with swirly patterns. It had two big wheels, and a little seat in front. Two long pull bars fitted perfectly into Mudlark's harness. The cart looked like a small pony trap.

"It's Mudlark's fish cart," said Dad. "Before Marjorie adopted Mudlark, he belonged to her brother, who used to sell and deliver fresh fish to the houses in town. That was years ago, before her brother went off, but Marjorie still uses the cart to collect her weekly shopping. Mudlark loves to pull it along and give rides, don't you, Mudlark?"

The little black donkey replied with a loud hee-haw.

"Would you like a ride, Emma?" said Dad.

"Oh, yes, please," said Emma. But first she took Sheltie's saddle off and slipped the bridle over his head. She laid them carefully over the top bar of the fence, then climbed into the cart.

Mom came out of the house with Joshua to watch.

Emma took Mudlark's long reins and Dad led the donkey around the paddock. Sheltie thought this was a lot of fun and trotted alongside. He tossed his head and swatted Emma with his swishing tail.

Once Emma was used to the reins, Dad let go and Emma drove the little fish cart around the paddock on her own, in a big circle.

Then Joshua wanted a ride. So Mom lifted him on to the seat next to Emma and Mudlark pulled them both along. Joshua gurgled with laughter as the little cart trundled around the paddock.

When the ride was over, Mom took Joshua inside and put a pizza in the oven for their snack.

Dad took Mudlark out of the harness

and wheeled the cart back behind Sheltie's field shelter. Then he went into the house to help Mom.

☆

Chapter Four

Emma stayed in the paddock for a while with Sheltie. She was about to put his saddle and bridle away when she noticed a man standing by the fence, talking to Mudlark. The man was scratching Mudlark's ears, and the donkey was enjoying every minute of it.

The man looked like the old gardener that Emma had seen earlier at Marjorie's cottage.

"Good afternoon, miss," said the man politely. "That's a fine donkey you have there. I could use a donkey like that."

Emma thought that was a funny thing to say. She made a face and said, "He doesn't belong to us. We're only taking care of him

for Marjorie Wallace while she's away."

"Oh," said the man with a smile. Then he touched his cap politely and said goodbye.

Emma watched the man walk away up the lane. Although she had never seen him before, Emma thought that the man looked very familiar. He reminded her of someone, but she couldn't think who.

Emma quickly put Sheltie's tack away, then rushed inside to tell Mom and Dad.

"It doesn't sound like Mr. Rudd, the gardener," said Dad. "Maybe it was the new handyman at Mr. Brown's place. He's doing some odd jobs around the farm."

"Well, I didn't like him," said Emma. "He wanted Mudlark."

"He was probably just being friendly," said Mom.

Dad put some pizza slices on plates, and Mom carried them to the kitchen table. They all sat down to eat.

Later that evening when Emma went up to bed, she lay awake thinking about the missing kitten. Emma wondered if Mrs. Marsh had found it yet. She decided to ride over again first thing in the morning and find out.

But the next morning Emma made a terrible discovery. When she went to the paddock, Mudlark was nowhere to be seen.

The paddock gate was locked and bolted, and there were no breaks in the fence or any holes where the donkey could have escaped. But Mudlark had gone. Emma ran back inside to fetch Mom.

Mom could hardly believe it. She went outside to see for herself.

Sheltie was tossing his head and dashing around the paddock.

"Do you know what happened, Sheltie?" said Mom. "Where's Mudlark?"

Sheltie stared up into the branches of an overhanging tree. He gave a loud snort and scraped at the grass with his hoof.

Emma glanced up into the tree and saw a man's cap hanging from one of the branches.

"How did that get up there?" Emma asked.

Mom went to get a broom. Then she reached up into the tree and knocked the cap off the branch.

When the cap fell to the ground, Sheltie rushed over and picked it up between his teeth. Then with a quick flick, he tossed it up into the air, just like a Frisbee.

"Did you throw it up there before, Sheltie?" said Mom.

"I think he must have," said Emma. "I bet whoever's taken Mudlark dropped it, and Sheltie tossed it up into the tree."

"We'd better tell Dad and call the police," said Mom.

☆

Chapter Five

Half an hour later, Officer Green arrived. He examined the paddock and chain and the bolt on the paddock gate, then scratched his head.

"And you say there's no trace of the donkey anywhere?"

Dad shook his head. "We've looked everywhere."

"And called him," said Mom. "He's definitely gone."

"Stolen," said Emma. "Someone's stolen him! I bet it was that man."

"We can't be sure of that yet, Emma," said the policeman.

He looked around the paddock again, checking the fence. But there were no clues to Mudlark's disappearance. Then Mom handed over the cap.

"We found this," she said. It was an ordinary brown checked cap.

"This could belong to anyone," said the policeman.

"I bet it belongs to the thief," said Emma.

"I'll report the incident and organize a

search," said the policeman. "But I guess if your donkey *has* been stolen, then he's miles away by now."

"Oh, no," said Mom. "What will we tell poor Marjorie?"

Officer Green looked out in the road for fresh tire tracks, but there were none. The weather had been nice for weeks, and the lane was dry and dusty.

There were no footprints, either. No hoof marks. No tire tracks. No clues at all. And no Mudlark.

"Sheltie must have seen who took Mudlark," said Emma.

Officer Green smiled. "But I'm afraid Sheltie can't tell us, can he, Emma?"

I bet he can, thought Emma. But she didn't say so.

When the policeman left to organize a search, Emma took another look around the paddock.

Mom and Dad went back inside the house. Mom looked very worried. Dad thought it was best not to telephone Marjorie just yet. He didn't want to spoil her vacation. He said they should wait a while and see if the police found Mudlark.

Out in the paddock, Sheltie was nosing around in the long grass by the gatepost. He pawed at the ground and kept pushing his muzzle into a clump of nettles.

Emma went over to see what Sheltie was so interested in.

Sheltie pushed his head forward into the long grass and gave a loud sneeze. Emma carefully parted the nettles. She found a

tiny scrap of red woolen cloth caught on a
bramble by the gatepost.

The scrap was no bigger than a postage
stamp. Emma took the piece of wool in to
show Mom and Dad.

"It could be a piece of sweater or a
scarf," said Mom. "But none of us has

anything that color. It's probably been there for ages, Emma."

But Emma didn't think so. She was certain that Sheltie didn't, either. They both thought it was a clue.

Emma put the red woolly scrap into her back pocket.

"I hope the policemen find Mudlark soon," said Emma. "What would the thieves do with him?"

"Well, he could end up anywhere," said Dad. "Probably in a market somewhere, to be sold as a working donkey."

"Oh, poor Mudlark," said Emma. "How awful. He's much too old to work. And he'll miss Marjorie." She was close to tears. And she kept thinking how horrible it would be if Sheltie had been stolen.

☆
Chapter Six

When Dad came home from work, everyone was sitting around the kitchen table. Emma and Joshua were drawing. All day at school Emma had thought about poor Mudlark. So far she had drawn eight pictures. They were all of donkeys.

Dad called the police station. They told him their search had found nothing. They had even been over to Mr. Brown's farm to question the new handyman. But the handyman had finished all the odd jobs around the place. He had even mended the old rusty lock on the cowshed. Mr. Brown had paid him and he had already gone on his way.

After tea, Emma decided to ride Sheltie over to Beacon Hill to visit Mrs. Marsh again. She was hoping that the kitten had turned up. But there was no such luck.

"I've been searching and searching," said Mrs. Marsh. "And I still can't find it. It's disappeared."

"Or been stolen," said Emma. She told Mrs. Marsh about Mudlark and the man she had seen hopping over the fence the previous day.

"It couldn't have been Mr. Rudd, the gardener. He's not due until tomorrow," said Mrs. Marsh. They both looked puzzled.

"I bet it was that man then," said Emma. "And I bet he's taken Mudlark *and* the kitten."

Mrs. Marsh didn't know what to think.

When Emma had to leave, she climbed into Sheltie's saddle and squeezed with her heels.

"Come on, Sheltie." And Sheltie trotted off. But he wouldn't go the way Emma wanted him to.

Sheltie turned around and went up the path toward the woods behind Marjorie's cottage.

Emma let Sheltie take the lead. They trotted along the path and into the woods.

Emma knew that Sheltie wanted to show her something. He kept his head high and sniffed at the wind as he went along.

A little way into the woods, they came to a clearing. Up ahead, sheltered by some overhanging trees, Emma saw a funny-looking trailer.

The trailer was tiny. It looked like a little garden shed on wheels.

Nearby, tied to a tree, were two donkeys. One donkey was gray and the other one was almost pure white. It looked like a ghost.

Sheltie sniffed at the air and both his ears pricked up.

Emma slipped out of the saddle. She and Sheltie were hidden from view by a thicket

of shrubs. They kept very quiet and watched as an old man came out of the trailer.

It was the same man that Emma had seen hopping over Marjorie's fence. And the same man who had spoken to her in the paddock. Emma was certain of it.

He did remind her of someone. But Emma *still* couldn't think who.

She held her breath and watched as the man untied the white donkey and led it away, off into the woods.

When he had gone, Emma crept out from her hiding place. Sheltie gave a snort and watched her tiptoe toward the trailer .

Behind the trailer, Emma found a clothesline strung out across two poles.

On the line was a shirt, a vest and a pair of red socks. Emma stared at the socks. Her eyes grew wide and her heart thumped in her chest.

The socks were the same color as the piece of woolly material that Sheltie had found by the paddock gate.

Emma took a closer look at the socks. And there, in one of them, was a tear. A hole no bigger than a postage stamp.

Emma took the piece of wool out of her pocket and held it up against the sock. The color matched perfectly. That meant that

the man who owned the socks had been in the paddock. And he must have stolen Mudlark!

As Emma stood by the trailer she thought she heard a cat meow. Emma listened carefully and pressed her ear against the painted wood. She heard the meow again. The sound was coming from inside the trailer.

Suddenly, a twig snapped in the woods. Emma jumped. The man was coming back. Sheltie gave a warning snort, and Emma ran back and jumped into the saddle.

She squeezed her heels and Sheltie took off, trotting back through the woods and along the path to Beacon Hill.

Chapter Seven

Emma decided to ride straight back home and tell Mom and Dad what she had discovered.

When she burst in through the kitchen door, Emma was red in the face and out of breath.

She told Mom and Dad all about the funny little trailer in the woods, the socks on the clothesline, and the cat crying.

When she had finished, Dad reached for the telephone to call Officer Green at the station again.

The policeman went to the woods behind Beacon Hill right away. But when he got there, the trailer was gone. There was no sign of it anywhere. No Mudlark and no tracks on the leafy forest floor.

Everyone was very disappointed.

"Maybe we should telephone Marjorie at her sister's and tell her what's happening," said Mom.

Officer Green thought they should wait a little while longer. The next day was Saturday, and there would be three markets in nearby towns. Maybe Mudlark would be put up for sale at one of them. Officer Green suggested they wait to see what happened.

"There's no point in causing unnecessary worry," he said. They all agreed.

"The markets start early in the morning, so we should know by noon if the thief is going to try to sell the little donkey."

That night, when she went to bed, Emma lay awake thinking about poor Mudlark. She wondered where he was, and kept thinking how sad and frightened he must be and how awful it would be for Marjorie when she found out that her donkey had been stolen.

When Emma finally fell asleep, she had

a bad dream. She dreamed that Sheltie had been stolen, and she was running all over Little Applewood looking for him. But she couldn't find him anywhere.

In the morning, Emma woke up suddenly and jumped out of bed. She ran over to look out of her bedroom window and breathed a sigh of relief. Sheltie was out there in the paddock as usual, looking over the wooden fence.

Everyone was quiet during breakfast.

Emma wasn't hungry at all and pushed her cereal around with her spoon.

All they could do was wait and see if Mudlark turned up at any of the markets.

☆ Chapter Eight

At twelve o'clock, Officer Green came to the house. There was still no sign of Mudlark. He hadn't been spotted at any one of the three markets.

"I'm afraid there's not much hope of finding him now," said the policeman.

"Maybe you should contact Mrs. Wallace after all."

Mom tried to call Marjorie, but there was no answer.

"They must have gone out," she said. "I'll try again later."

Emma thought she would take Sheltie out for a ride over to Beacon Hill again. She wanted to check with Mrs. Marsh to see if the missing kitten had found its way home. Emma kept thinking about the meowing she had heard from inside the trailer. She was almost certain that it was the kitten.

Emma talked to Sheltie as she plopped the saddle on to his back.

"Do you know where Mudlark is, Sheltie?"

Sheltie tilted his head to one side, listening.

As Emma strapped the leather girth under his fat tummy, she said, "I bet if anyone can find Mudlark, you can."

By the time she had fitted the bridle and sat up in the saddle holding the reins, Sheltie was eager to set off.

Emma rode Sheltie out of the paddock and squeezed her heels to send him trotting down the road.

But Sheltie didn't want to go that way and headed off in the opposite direction. Emma let the reins go slack, and Sheltie took the lead.

"Are we going to find Mudlark, Sheltie?" asked Emma. Sheltie blew from his nostrils and quickened his pace.

They crossed Mr. Brown's meadow, and

rode past Horseshoe Pond to the back field. There Bramble Woods began and swept back in a wide arc all the way across to Beacon Hill. The woods were much thicker at that end, and led off, up and over the hills and beyond.

Sheltie carried on, following the bridle path into the woods. They both knew that track very well. Emma knew that the thickest part of the wood lay up ahead.

As they climbed the rise, Emma looked back and saw Mr. Brown's farm nestling in the fields below. It was the perfect spot for looking out across the countryside and all of Little Applewood.

As they reached the top, the trees grew thicker and the ground leveled out. Sheltie left the track and headed into the deepest

part of the woods.

They hadn't gone far when Emma gasped. Up ahead, beneath the trees, was the little trailer. Two donkeys were harnessed to the trailer's pull bars. The gray one and the ghostly white one.

Sheltie stopped and Emma slid out of the saddle. Sheltie let out an excited snort. "Shh," whispered Emma. She pressed a finger to her lips.

They hid behind a big bush and watched. There was no sign of anyone.

Then Emma heard someone whistling, and she saw the old man stepping out of the trailer. He was walking straight toward them. Emma held her breath and whispered to Sheltie to keep still.

Chapter Nine

The man walked straight past them, just ten yards away. He kept whistling and followed the path down the hill through the woods. He was carrying an empty plastic container. Emma guessed that he was heading for the stream to get some water.

Emma and Sheltie watched the man disappear through the trees.

When it was safe to come out of hiding, Emma left the bush and approached the trailer. Sheltie gave a snort and followed.

As soon as the ghostly white donkey saw Emma and Sheltie, it threw back its head with a loud hee-haw just like Mudlark.

Sheltie rushed over and nuzzled the white donkey with his nose as though he were greeting a long-lost friend. The donkey's long ears stood straight up and Sheltie began licking them.

Emma watched as the donkey's ears turned from white to black. Suddenly Emma realized that it *was* Mudlark. He had been covered from head to hoof with white flour!

Emma looked around and wondered what to do next. Then she heard a meow. It's the kitten, she thought.

The sound was coming from inside the trailer. Emma reached for the trailer door and turned the handle. The little door swung open and Emma stepped inside.

The trailer was very small and very messy. There were clothes thrown everywhere, a jumble of old newspapers, and things packed in cardboard boxes. Emma saw a brown checked jacket scrunched up in a ball on the low bunk bed. It was the same color and pattern as the cap that Sheltie had tossed into the tree.

Curled up in the middle of the jacket was an old gray tabby cat. Not the missing kitten after all. The cat opened one lazy green eye and meowed.

Outside, Sheltie was becoming very agitated. He gave a snort and scraped at the ground with his hoof. He was shaking his head and blowing loudly.

The man was coming back. Emma peeked through the only window in the back of the trailer and saw him walking back up the path.

It was too late to run. The man would see her. Clever Sheltie had gone deeper into the woods and was standing behind a clump of bushes. Emma pulled the trailer door closed and stayed inside. She quickly looked around for somewhere to hide.

Luckily, she noticed a space under the bed and crawled into it.

The trailer door opened and the old man stepped inside. He sat down on the bunk and the bed springs groaned, inches above Emma's head.

Emma could see the man's feet and legs in front of her. He was wearing the red socks, the ones with the hole in them. Emma could see the hole quite clearly. It

was just above his shoe. Her heart beat
faster and faster.

★ Chapter Ten

A few minutes passed by. It seemed like hours. The man was talking to the cat, which was purring loudly.

"What a pity we missed Marji, Tigger! Never mind. Maybe we'll see her next time we're passing through. I hope Marji doesn't mind too much about Mudlark. I felt mean taking him like that, but those nice people would never have just handed him over."

Then the man got up and went outside. He locked the door behind him and Emma heard him climb up into the driving seat at the front of the trailer.

She heard a jangling of reins and the man called out, "Giddy-up!" The trailer slowly rolled forward and bumped across the uneven ground, with Emma inside.

Emma crawled out from under the bed. She peered out of the window and saw Sheltie peeping from behind the thicket, watching as the trailer pulled away.

The trailer was heading up to the open field toward the main road.

Sheltie gave a snort and flicked his tail. Emma didn't know what to do. She looked at Sheltie and waved her hands. Get help, Sheltie, she thought. Go and get help. And Sheltie turned and galloped away, just as though he had understood.

Sheltie was a very smart pony. He knew that Emma was in trouble. He wanted to follow the trailer, but it might be better to bring help.

Sheltie galloped as fast as he could, crashing through the woods along the bridle path back down to Little Applewood.

Sheltie knew the path very well. Every dip and turn. His little legs covered the distance quickly.

Sheltie headed for home. He crossed Mr. Brown's meadow and was soon galloping up the lane to the house.

Mom and Dad were in the kitchen with Joshua, talking about Marjorie and poor Mudlark. They still hadn't been able to reach her by telephone.

Sheltie came trotting in through the open kitchen door. His hooves clattered on the polished floor tiles.

Mom jumped up out of her chair with a start. Joshua giggled as Dad caught hold of Sheltie's reins.

"Whoa, Sheltie," said Dad. "Where's Emma?"

Mom took Sheltie outside to see if Emma was in the paddock. Sometimes Sheltie slipped away from Emma just for fun. Dad came outside with Joshua. They saw that Emma was nowhere around. Dad called her.

"Emma! Emma!"

There was no reply.

"Something must have happened," said Mom.

"Emma told me she was going over to visit Mrs. Marsh. I'll give her a call." Mom hurried inside and picked up the telephone.

Mrs. Marsh said she hadn't seen Emma all day long. But she told Mom that she would walk the footpath to the top of Beacon Hill and look for her. You could see for miles up there.

Outside, Sheltie was getting impatient. He stamped the ground with his feet and shook his mane. Then he ran off a little way toward the paddock and stopped, looking back at Mom and Dad standing outside the house.

"He wants us to follow him," said Mom.

Sheltie trotted into the paddock and disappeared behind his field shelter. When

Mom and Dad got there, Sheltie was standing between the pull bars of Mudlark's little fish cart. He was blowing and snorting like crazy.

"I think he wants you to go with him in the cart," said Mom. They both knew that Sheltie was trying to help.

Chapter Eleven

Dad quickly slipped Mudlark's special harness over Sheltie and fitted the pull bars of the fish cart in place.

"Let Sheltie take you to Emma," said Mom. "I'll stay here with Joshua and call the police."

"But how will you know where we're heading?" said Dad.

"I'll watch and see which way you go," said Mom.

Dad jumped into the fish cart and Sheltie was off. Mom watched as Sheltie pulled the cart out of the paddock, down the road, and across Mr. Brown's meadow, heading for the back field and Bramble Woods.

Sheltie was only a little Shetland pony, but he was very strong for his size. He pulled the fish cart all the way up the rise where the trees grew thicker and the ground leveled out.

Sheltie didn't stop once. He pulled the cart along the track through the woods and out on to the edge of the open fields.

A high ridge swept around and across to Beacon Hill. Mrs. Marsh was up there looking for Emma. She stood by the side of the path as Sheltie trotted up with Dad in the cart.

Mrs. Marsh looked surprised.

"Any sign of Emma?" asked Dad.

"I'm afraid not," said Mrs. Marsh. "But I saw a funny little trailer a moment ago, crossing the clearing over there." She pointed toward a low, rolling slope a short distance away.

"Two donkeys pulling a little trailer," she said. "Only minutes ago. It must be heading for the main road."

The little fish cart flew along. Sheltie galloped as fast as his legs could carry him. The cart bumped down the rolling slope

and on to the field.

Up ahead, they could see the trailer and the gray road beyond. As they drew nearer, Dad suddenly saw Emma peering out through the trailer window. He was so surprised that he stood up . . . and fell out of the cart. He landed on the grass with a bump, but he was unhurt.

Sheltie looked back, but he didn't stop.

He could go faster now without Dad's weight in the cart, so he galloped on, and soon he was level with the trailer.

The driver was very surprised to see a Shetland pony appear out of nowhere. And even more surprised when Sheltie overtook the two donkeys and stopped suddenly in front of the moving trailer.

The donkeys stopped dead in their tracks, and the trailer came to a sudden halt.

The old man jangled the reins and yelled, "Giddy-up, Mudlark, Sophie." But the donkeys didn't move. Instead, Mudlark just threw back his head and gave a loud hee-haw!

Chapter Twelve

Everything seemed to happen at once. A police car came roaring down the main road. Mom had told the police that Sheltie was heading in that direction. The police car screeched to a halt when the trailer had been spotted. Officer Green jumped out.

Dad was also on his feet and ran up alongside. He pulled open the trailer door, and Emma stepped out.

The man just sat there holding the limp reins.

"Where on earth did *she* come from?" He could hardly believe his own eyes. He suddenly looked very worried.

Emma ran into Dad's arms.

"I think you've got some explaining to do," said Officer Green.

"Oh dear," said the man. "I never meant any harm. I had no idea that the little girl was inside." The old man was very confused.

"It's true," said Emma. "He didn't know I was in there." Emma thought the man looked very sad. And close up he had a kind face.

Emma suddenly knew who he reminded her of. He looked just like Marjorie Wallace.

Sheltie began to give Mudlark a bath. He was licking the little donkey all over. And the more he cleaned the white donkey, the more the real black donkey showed through.

"A clever trick, covering the donkey in flour," said Officer Green. "But you didn't fool Sheltie."

Sheltie gave a loud snort when he heard his name.

"I'm going to arrest you for stealing this animal," said the policeman. "Do you have anything to say for yourself?"

The old man looked ashamed and lowered his head.

"I'm very sorry," he said. "But I didn't really steal him. I was just taking him back."

"Taking him back? What do you mean?" asked Dad.

The old man said he was Todd Wallace, Marjorie's brother.

So that's why he looks so much like Marjorie, thought Emma.

Todd explained how, years ago, he used to sell and deliver fresh fish to the people in Little Applewood.

"Mudlark and Sophie are brother and sister, too," he said. "I used Mudlark to pull that very same fish cart through the streets.

"When I went off on my travels I left Mudlark behind with Marji. He was too frisky for a trailer, and I couldn't take care of two donkeys. And Marji did say that I could have Mudlark back whenever I wanted. She always knew I would come back for him one day."

"But that was a long time ago," said Officer Green. "And why didn't you tell

Marjorie you were coming back for him and just *ask* instead of taking the donkey like that?"

Todd said that Marjorie was always trying to make him give up his life on the road.

"She wants me to settle down and live in a real house," he said. "I had come to ask, but when I found out that Marji was away, I thought it would be much easier just to take Mudlark and explain later." He looked at Emma and then at Dad.

"I know that it was wrong to take Mudlark from your paddock," said Todd. "But I only wanted Sophie to have some company in her old age. And a little help to pull the trailer." He looked really sad.

"Well, what you say may be true, but

you'll have to stay at the police station until Marjorie gets back and we clear up this mess," said the policeman.

"One thing still bothers me, though," said Emma. "If you weren't stealing Mudlark, why did you try to disguise him by covering him in flour?"

Todd lowered his head.

"I knew everyone would be looking for Mudlark. And I thought that if I disguised him then I could get away quietly without any fuss. I'm very sorry for all the trouble I've caused. I really am."

Officer Green drove Todd away in the back of the police car.

Chapter Thirteen

Dad said he would take care of the trailer, Sophie, and Tigger, the cat. He climbed up into the driver's seat and took the reins. Slowly he turned Mudlark and Sophie around. Then he drove the caravan back up the slope to the top of the rise.

Emma followed behind in the fish cart, with Sheltie pulling it. Sheltie liked the little cart, and Emma thought it was fantastic to steer with the long reins.

They met Mrs. Marsh on the crest of the hill. She seemed quite surprised to see Dad driving the trailer, with Emma and Sheltie following behind in the painted fish cart. She gave them a friendly wave and a big smile as they passed.

When they crossed Mr. Brown's meadow and drove up the road, little Joshua could hardly believe his eyes. He was waiting with Mom at the front gate, staring wide-eyed with amazement.

Once safely in the paddock, Dad freed Mudlark and Sophie from the trailer.

Emma unharnessed Sheltie from the fish

cart, then went inside to get a bucket of warm water from the kitchen.

She went to work with soap and a soft brush, and soon Mudlark was back to his normal color, as black as coal.

Sheltie galloped around the paddock, chasing Sophie and Mudlark in a game of

tag. Mom went inside for some carrots and apples.

"What's going to happen to Mr. Wallace?" asked Emma. "Will he go to prison? And who will take care of Sophie?"

"I don't think he'll go to prison, seeing that he's Marjorie's brother, Emma. He did seem like a nice man. And if what he said about Mudlark is true, then I guess he didn't really steal the donkey anyway. But it was a silly thing to do. We'll have to wait until Marjorie gets back and see what she has to say. In the meantime, there's plenty of room in the paddock. That is, if Sheltie doesn't mind!"

Sheltie shook his mane and let out a long blow. He didn't mind at all.

A few days later, Marjorie came back from her vacation. Emma's dad picked her up from the train station and drove her home in the car.

When he sat Marjorie down and told her all the news, she could hardly believe her ears.

"Who would have thought that old Todd would turn up like that!" she said. "I often think of him and wonder what he's up to, traveling around in that funny trailer all the time. He never did like living in one place in a real house, like the rest of us. And he carries all his precious papers and things around in a silly old sack so he doesn't lose them."

Marjorie was very worried about her brother being held at the police station.

She asked Dad if he would drive her there right away. She wanted to clear up this mess as quickly as possible.

Chapter Fourteen

That afternoon, Marjorie called the house and asked if Emma and Sheltie would ride over after school. She said that she had some good news.

When Emma and Sheltie arrived, Marjorie was sitting out in the garden with her nine cats. She was very pleased to see Emma.

"You are such a clever girl, Emma," she said. "And Sheltie is such a clever pony."

Marjorie had been told all about Emma and Sheltie's adventure and how they tracked down and found Mudlark.

"It was Sheltie really," said Emma. "He found all the clues—the cap and the piece of sock—and he led me to the trailer and Mudlark."

"Oh yes, I mustn't forget," said Marjorie, "I've got a special present for Sheltie." She went inside and came back with a beautiful leather saddle. It shone like a chestnut.

"This saddle used to belong to Mudlark. But nobody rides him any more. Todd gave me the saddle along with Mudlark and the little painted fish cart over ten years ago when he left. I think it will be just right for Sheltie. It was Todd's idea."

"Oh, thank you. It's perfect," said Emma. "I'll save it for special occasions. It can be Sheltie's dress-up saddle."

Sheltie sniffed at the leather and blew a loud snort of approval. He liked the dress-up saddle very much. Emma and Marjorie

laughed. Sheltie could be so funny at times.

"What will happen to your brother?" asked Emma. "And Sophie?"

Marjorie gave a big sigh.

"I'm afraid Todd is getting too old to go off on his travels any more. I've sorted everything out with the police. And I told Todd that Mudlark's and Sophie's trailer-pulling days are over, and that he's got to settle down."

"Will he come and live here in Little Applewood?" asked Emma.

Sheltie pricked up his ears.

"I hope so," said Marjorie. "Or one of the nearby towns."

"And will he take Mudlark?"

"That's the good news, Emma. Todd said I can have Mudlark for keeps. And

Sophie, too. I told Todd he will be able to come and visit them whenever he wants. But I hope he decides to come and live here with me. And I hope you and Sheltie will come and visit too, Emma."

Sheltie pushed his muzzle into Marjorie's hand and blew hot air up her sleeve.

"That would be great," laughed Emma.

"And we've found the missing kitten too," said Marjorie. "He'd gone and locked himself inside the toolshed."

Everything had turned out fine after all.

Mudlark and Sophie were in their little field behind Marjorie's cottage. Sheltie trotted over on his own and rubbed noses with the two donkeys.

"You're very lucky to have such a clever pony, Emma," said Marjorie.

"I know," said Emma. "Sheltie's the best pony in the world."

Everyone needs Kitten Friends™!

Fluffy and fun, purry and huggable, what could be more perfect than a kitten?

by
Jenny Dale

ALADDIN PAPERBACKS
Simon & Schuster Children's Publishing
www.SimonSaysKids.com